PRAISE FOR

# WHEN YOU KNOW WHAT I KNOW

"Written with leap-off-the page boldness and sensitivity,
Sonja K. Solter's *When You Know What I Know* is as **fresh
and profound** a story of hope in the aftermath of tragedy
as I have ever read. Young readers will hang on to every
word of Tori's confusion, pain, and hard-won
renewal. **A triumph!**"
—Tony Abbott, author of *The Summer of Owen Todd*
and *The Great Jeff*

"A difficult but **important read**, giving a voice
to sexual abuse survivors and helping others see
the complexity of emotions and the hard work
that goes into the healing process."
—*School Library Journal*

"The book is **smart**."
—*The Bulletin*

"This **offering of hope** after trauma is,
manticized."
*views*

WHEN YOU
KNOW WHAT
I KNOW

# WHEN YOU
# KNOW WHAT
# I KNOW

## SONJA K. SOLTER

LITTLE, BROWN AND COMPANY
New York  Boston

Little, Brown and Company
Hachette Book Group
1290 Avenue of the Americas, New York, NY 10104
Visit us at LBYR.com

Originally published in hardcover and ebook by
Little, Brown and Company in March 2020
First Trade Paperback Edition: March 2021

Little, Brown and Company is a division of Hachette Book Group, Inc.
The Little, Brown name and logo are trademarks of
Hachette Book Group, Inc.

The publisher is not responsible for websites (or their content)
that are not owned by the publisher.

The Library of Congress has cataloged the hardcover as follows:
Names: Solter, Sonja K., author.
Title: When you know what I know / by Sonja Solter.
Description: First edition. | New York ; Boston : Little, Brown and Company, 2020. | Summary: Over the course of a year, ten-year-old Tori endures a difficult and emotional journey after revealing that she has been sexually abused by her uncle.
Identifiers: LCCN 2019013415| ISBN 9780316535441 (hardcover) | ISBN 9780316535410 (ebook) | ISBN 9780316535434 (library edition ebook)
Subjects: | CYAC: Novels in verse. | Sexual abuse—Fiction. | Single-parent families—Fiction. | Schools—Fiction.
Classification: LCC PZ7.5.S64 Whe 2020 | DDC [Fic]—dc23
LC record available at https://lccn.loc.gov/2019013415

ISBNs: 978-0-316-53542-7 (pbk.), 978-0-316-53541-0 (ebook)

Printed in the United States of America

LSC-C

**Printing 1, 2021**

For all the healing journeys, both told and as-yet-untold

# PROLOGUE

# TELLING

When you know
what I know,
you'll wish you
didn't.

It's not the kind
of thing you can
talk about
at school or
at the park
or anywhere,
with a new friend
or an old one
or even with your sister.
(She's too little.)

But it's everywhere
once you know,

once you can't
not know.
In your face,
under your eyelids.
If you turn
your back on it,

there it is anyway.

# PART ONE

# THAT FACE

I keep catching a glimpse of
That Face in the mirror,
That Face from right after,
locked in the bathroom,
after He was gone,
praying Mom would just
get back, come home.
And I want to shat-
ter the glass shat-
ter That Face haunt-
ing me with her
dead eyes.

And never
have to see
That Face
again,
That Face
that is mine.

# BELIEVE ME

She didn't believe me.
She—
my Mom, Mommy, Mama—
she said,
Oh!
—no.
Uncle Andy?
Didn't believe me.
No—no, he
wouldn't do that.
Didn't believe me.
Honey, you must have
misunderstood.
You know how he
plays around,
how goofy he is—
just like you.

And it was like she put
a pillow over my
brain and I couldn't—
couldn't breathe,
couldn't think anymore.
Was it—was it
possible? Did I—
DID I misunderstand?

And then a whooshing-wave-
of-fire-and-ice-cold
roared up my legs and
out my ears and blew
off the top of my head.

Believe me.

      Please...

         Believe me.

But she didn't.

# TRAPPED

I sit,
pasted to my bed
stuffed with a hush
that drowns my mind.

I stare;
the red curtain folds
flick-flick-flickering
above the heater vent.

I blink;
metal wires pop out
at me: the cage
next to my desk.

Suddenly its bars trap me
inside the memory

that floods my mind as if
it's happening right now—

> Chittering laughs of children
> at my eighth birthday party.
> Nestling softness in my palms;
> Uncle Andy's deep booming voice.
> His hands cup mine, giving me
> the best present of all time:
> a hamster.

I standupwalkovercrouchdown
alittlenosepokingsniffingsmelling
through the metal wire.
And I reach out
—not to her—
to the door
in the middle
the one we NeverEver
Open.

# NOT ONE WORD

Rhea and I tell
each other
everything.
Always have.
And here she is
sitting next to me
at lunch on Tuesday.
Rhea who told me
when she got her period
so young, even though
she looked like she
wanted to die.

But I don't know
what to do
what to do
what to do.
It's too hard

to say
even
one
word.

So I just chew my lip
and don't talk to my
best friend until she
gets in a huff
and leaves to
sit at another table.
And I chew and chew and chew—
but not my food.

# THE TEST

What if I hadn't gone down to the basement?

(He said not to follow him down there. He said that.)

What if I'd stopped wrestling around last year?

(Back when Mom said, *Aren't you getting too old for
    that?*)

What if I hadn't tickled him on the tummy that other
    time?

What if I'd gone over to Rhea's that day?

What if I hadn't laughed at first?
What if he didn't really mean it like that?
What if he thought that's what I wanted?
What if I'd told him to knock it off?

What if these What-Ifs are right?

What if I'm wrong?

What if I'm just paranoid?

What if it's—what if—it's me—what if I—what

if I made a—what if it was a mistake?

What if what if what if

what if what if what if what if

what if what if what if what if what if what

if what if what if what if what if what if what if

what if what if what if what if what if w

hat if what if what if what if what if wha

t if what if what if what if what if what i

f what if what if what if what if what if w

hat if what if what if whatif whatif whatif

whatif whatif whatifwhatifwhat—


*Class, put your pencils down.*


I watch my test packet

shuffle forward

row by row

to Mr. Jenkins's desk.

Somewhere in that huge pile

of papers:

my blank one.

# GHOST GIRL

*What are we, six?*
Rhea uncaps a glue stick
and adds final touches
to her Halloween decoration.

I nod, which some part of me
knows doesn't make sense.
But I'm not really listening to her
usual wanting-to-be-older talk.
A white noise hum
purrs away
inside me.
I let it lull me away from
everything out there.

*Class 5J: preparing us for kindergarten
instead of middle school.*

Now Rhea's frowning at me
so I'd better say something.

Otherwise she might ask me
What's Wrong.

(And I can't tell her.)

I point to her wispy ghost girl.
*Yours looks good, though.*

*Yeah, I'll admit*
*I kind of like her.*
Rhea lifts her up and
whooshes her shredded
tissue skirt around.

The hum inside gets
more intense,
pulling me back.

But.

I lift up whatever it is that
I made. A ghost too, I guess.

Rhea's eyes widen.
*Whoa, yours looks—*
*Modern? Abstract?*

*Dead,* I say.

Rhea nods. *That's appropriate.*

# MONSTERS

*Are you sure?*
*Are you sure*
*you don't want to*
*dress up this year?*
*Go trick-or-treating?*

Mom drops the fabric
onto the counter,
the shimmery blue fabric
I chose six months ago:
shimmery blue because
I'd decided to be a genie,
six months ago because
Halloween is was
my favorite holiday.

I lie and tell her
my friends aren't dressing up

this year.
I channel Rhea:
too babyish,
too last-year.

Her gaze lowers,
disappointed eyes
look down at the fabric,
hands smooth it.

*But you love Halloween.*

*Used to*—I *used to love it,* I say,
which is the truth.
Then I shrug like I don't care,
and the shrug is a lie.

I don't tell her
that people dressing up
to be different
to be not-themselves
to be monsters
just doesn't sound fun
anymore.

# CHOIR

Thursday after school,
has it only been
three days?
Three days
since It
happened.

Now, sounds
scratch at
my brain.
Everyone's ~~singing~~
yelling.
The piano clanks
and clunks
and the soprano next to me
screeches.

My hands itch to
cover my ears

but Ms. Radkte
glances my way
so I force my lips
to move instead.

Then the hum is there—
here in me—
filling me up
with its emptiness.
I keep moving my lips
with the now-muted song.
The world has gone
silent
like my voice.

The vibrations of the piano
of the singers
shake my feet
rattle my bones
but they don't reach me
anymore—
not really.

So much silence in
all that noise.

# BREAK

Mom's distracted,
lost in her checkbook,
cheeks sucking in
from unhappy surprises
at every other number
in front of her.
*He's late with child support again!*
she announces.

Perfect time to slip this in:
*I'm thinking about taking a break*
*from choir.*

Mom pauses, unfocused eyes
only half with me.
*Because of homework,* I rush on.
*Just for a little while.*

*Well.* She blows a strand of hair
off her cheek. *It's your decision.*
*We can't afford a sitter but*
*I guess I could ask Grandma*
*and Uncle Andy*
*if either of them could stay*
*for a couple of hours on*
*Tuesdays and Thursdays.*
*Thank God THEY'RE reliable.*

Her gaze is already back
on the checkbook as
everything goes cold,
colder. The hum buzzes
angrily in my head,
frantic to save me from
her words echoing
inside my skull:
*Uncle Andy*
*Uncle Andy*
*Uncle Andy . . .*

I stumble backward
into a chair, and

my ankle screams pain
at me from somewhere
outside the cold,
from somewhere
far below...

I hear myself babbling:
—*just thinking about it—probably*
*won't. I'm not sure yet. About*
*the break.*

The word "break"
is magic.
As I say it
the cold pierces
my mind, numbing
the buzz to stillness,
shattering my thoughts
into icicle pieces that
fall down and
away from here.

# THE COLD

I plunge in-
-to a deeper
cold, a freezing
lake, the ice
layer block-
-ing me from Mom,
from what she said.

*I don't want you to worry
about money,*
Mom calls after me
as I somehow
make it past
the chair.
*I shouldn't have said that
about your dad.
He'll get me his checks.
He always does.*

*Your dad's just busy with the*
*new baby and all.*


But her voice
can't reach me now.


There's a thump that might
be my arm hitting
the hallway wall,
a shush of covers
pulling over my head.


The icy lake keeps on
         sucking me
                  down

                        down

                           down

                              numbing

                                    me

                           saving

                              me.

# MISSING

Mom frowns at me,
one hand on the vacuum handle, her other
    pulling the chair away from my desk.
*Why isn't Furball in her cage?*

        I don't say anything.
        My Voice
        My Brain
        My Self
        are still

Missing

# MISSING, ROUND TWO

I push mashed potatoes
round and round with my fork,
Taylor's sobbing
filling my ears.
*Furball*, she moans.
*I miss he-e-er*, she wails.
I don't say that Tay
never
even
played with her, I just
smash and
squash peas.
Pressure on my shoulder—
Mom looms—
but I don't look up.
*I know it's not the same*,
she says, *but if we don't*
*find her, maybe we can*

*get another hamster.*
*Maybe even a—*
*Dog?* Taylor cuts in,
suddenly bright-eyed
and breathless.
*Rabbit,* Mom finishes.
She's not looking at Tay.
She's staring at me
like she's waiting
for some answer.
So I shrug
and start stabbing
the tofu.

# MY VOICE

Ms. Radtke frowns
at me because
I'm not singing.

Everyone can tell
when she's angry.
Her voice gets all
strained and shrieky,
like she swallowed
a mad cat.
*Ms. Radtke is Madtke,*
whispers into my ear.
It's Tilda, a popular girl
from Class 5S who likes
to giggle with me sometimes.
But I don't smile
at this old joke I made up

so long it seems like
forever ago.

I move my lips a little,
mumble-mouthing
random words.

*Okay, everyone grab an instrument!*
Out come:
the hand drums
some of the kids
start beating the
life out of, and
those tinkly things whose
chiming grates on me
like Taylor's nonstop babble
when I'm in a super bad mood.

Ms. Radtke tries
to hand me
a tambourine,
this scraped-up
tambourine,

but my arms are
anchored to my sides,
and it's all I can do
not to snatch away
Josh Lin's maracas
so he will just Shut Up!
and Ms. Radtke keeps
trying to give me
that tambourine,
shoving it at me
as she looks away to
tell off a drum-banger.

And then
right when
all the music



stops

My Voice bursts out
zero to a
**THOUSAND**
in a split second:

*I DONT WANT*
*THAT*
**DUMB**
*TAMBOURINE!*

Tori! yells Ms. Radtke.
*Yikes,* says Tilda.

But My Voice has gone
back into hiding.

# LIAR

I'm hidden under covers
and no one can get me out.
Not Mom.
Not breakfast.
Not Taylor.
Not lunch.

But Mom slips into my room
so quick and quiet
I can't even pretend
to be invisible,
like when I was younger
and she and Dad were
screaming at each other.

*Tori,* her voice whispers
close, her warm breath
wafting over my ear.

But something's different
about her presence,
something heavy
and focused on me,
a planet whose
gravity pulls me
up to sitting.
Tori, she says again,
her voice cracking,
urgent.
*Uncle Andy called today*
*to say*
*that he's worried about you*
*because—*
I'm frozen solid,
can't cover my ears
*—he says you've been lying*
*about things,*
*that you took a dollar from his wallet,*
*then told him you didn't when he asked.*
My stomach lurches, and the room
tilts along with it.
Mom puts a cool hand,
gentle,

on my chin,
turns my face toward her.
But I know you wouldn't do that,
and—a muscle twitches in her jaw—
I've always been able to tell
when Andrew's lying.

You've been so withdrawn lately,
looking sad, not liking
Halloween and choir . . .
Will you tell me
        again
what happened?

# TELLING, AGAIN

My throat closes up
and I can't speak,
can't say—
can't say—
IT—
all over again.

And then—
oh then—
she looks right into
my eyes,
and she—
my Mom, Mommy, Mama—
she sees the words
written there.
She finally SEES.

And she makes a noise,
a gulped sob,
like she's the one
strangling
instead of me.

# PART TWO

# ALIEN

Even when I don't see
Her anymore,
That Face from right after,
I still don't look
the same.
I look
in the mirror
and I think,
Who's That?

Now I look at
my arm—
not in the mirror,
right on me,
right at it.
And I still think,
Who's That?

And it's like a night
a few years ago.
I'd walked into my
parents' room
(back when Dad
still lived with us)
because I'd had a
nightmare.

But then I didn't
wake them up.

They looked so different
lying there,
not like themselves.
All waxy and still,
not smiling or frowning,
just blank-faced.
And then I got all freaked out
and remembered
a body-snatcher movie
and figured
that might have happened
to Mom and Dad.
So I scooted on back

to my room
real fast
because the monsters
in there
were less scary
than my alien parents.

So yeah,
my arm's like that.
And I keep pinching it,
but it's like the pain's
not connected to
the pinch.
Like my arm's not
connected to my
body.
Or maybe,
my whole body
is taken over,
and my mind has the
hurt on Earth,
but my body's
back on the home planet
with the alien
who's taken it over.

# NOO!!!

Nonononononononononono-

-nonononononononononono!

I don't want my teacher to know.

I don't want anyone to know.

Mr. Jenkins left a message, Tori.
You should have told me
you were having trouble
at school, honey.
I need to call him back right away.
Outbursts, failing tests:
he wants to know
What
is going on.

Mom, no!
No way!
No meeting!
I'm not going!

Fine, Mom snaps.
Then her lips relax.
I'll just tell him, Tori.
You don't have to be there.
She comes toward me,
arms open,
but I leap away.
No!

What? What are you talking about?
Tay pipes up,
eyes still glued to
her Pokémon movie.

Shut up! I shout.
Tay, go to your room, says Mom.
What'd I do? asks Taylor.
I need to talk to Tori, says Mom.

But Taylor's already gone
SLAMMING
her way out
of the kitchen (like she does
so we know how mad she is).
Well, so what? She has
NOTHING
to be mad about.


Mom!!!!! I screech. Mommy!


And I stomp wild all over—
You can't-can't-can't-can't!—
like that little two-year-old
from across the street
who Mom always calls
a real handful.


But she says we have
to tell Mr. Jenkins.
What do you want me to do, Tori?
Her eyes plead with me.
But I refuse to answer.
And her eyes shift,

determined now.
She goes into her bedroom and
I can hear her voice low in there,

Telling him.
Telling him
all about me.

So now I can't go to school tomorrow.

# THE NEXT MORNING

*Wake up, sweetie, c'mon.*

The sheet strips off from the
bare skin of my arms and legs and I
wrap my arms tight around my chest.

*He doesn't know much, Tori.*
*Just the very basics, no details.*
*He was very nice about it.*
*And he knows you're embarrassed,*
*so he won't talk to you about it*
*unless you bring it up.*

What?! She told him I'm embarrassed?!

Mom tries to roll me over but I
stick my face in the pillow instead,

smother myself in its mushy
sweatiness from the night.

*Tori, you can't let this*
*ruin your education.*
*You have your whole life*
*ahead of you, sweetie.*

With every wheedling
word,
I stuff my face farther
down,
down into the soft damp.

*You don't want to end up like me, right?*
(Stuff)
*Stuck with Mr. Hadley for a boss,*
(Stuff)
*and no way to get a better job?*
Her tone's light
but this is
NOT FUNNY.

Then—

*You don't want the bad stuff to win, right, sweetie?*

I bolt upright.

I just mean—Mom looks a little scared.
She tucks her head back, blinks a lot.
I mean you can't
let it win—
you won't!

She says this last
part like a cheerleader:
Go-get-'em, Tori!

But I glare at her, fierce,
so she knows.
Knows how much I hate her.
Laser-beam it from my eyes
so she can
feel it, not just see it.
Yank my robe off my desk chair.
Make for the bathroom.

SLAM!
the door good and hard
so she knows she is
Shut
Out.

# SCHOOL

I slip into Class 5J
shoot straight
past a smiling Rhea
to my cubby
shove my things in
spear my jacket
on its big fat hook.

And there's Mr. Jenkins.

*Hello, Tori. Welcome to class,*
he says,
which is what he always
says, but
it's still hard to look up at him,
so I stare down at his scuffed black
dress shoes,
his face

there in my mind
staring at me
as if he knows.

Because he does.

And later when Ms. Radtke
comes to get us for music,
I hear them whisper and
I'm sure it's me
they're glancing over at
while we get our notebooks,
while we line up.

And in the hall
as my class
jumbles its way
to music,
Ms. Radtke has
a word with
the gym teacher
right next door.
Their eyes go all
directions at once,

but I can tell they are
looking only at
Me.

And I'm sure they all
Know.

# LITTLE FISH

We went to Oakdale Pond today
to feed the fish.

Because it is Sunday,
and that's what we do on Sundays
ever since Dad left.
In the summer and early fall,
it's our special family time.

Even now.

I crumpled my baggie
of crumbs, squeezed
it, rolled it, first in one
palm, then the other.
The plastic slipped and
slid against itself until my crumbs
were little grains of nothing.

I held the baggie up to my eye.
I could see through my crumbs,
now too tiny to feed even
the smallest hungry little fish.
And there were Mom and Taylor
on the other side of the plastic.
Wavy and unreal,
like they were underwater.

*Tori! You ruined your crumbs!* Mom said.
Then she bit her lip.
*Have some of mine.*

*Hey, no fair. Give me some too,* said my sister
in her most irritating Taylor whine.

But Mom didn't even hear her.

I was already staring into the water,
and it took too much effort to
lift my head back up.

I threw some of Mom's bread crumbs down
into a group of the little white fish
who never gobble them fast enough.

But, of course,
one of the giant orange ones
barreled through and
the crumb-dots disappeared
before I could blink.

It's not like I could do anything about it.
I was up here, and they were way down there.

# THE FIRST TIME

Mom asks me
her voice stum-
bling, *Did he
do this—did he
touch you
before?*

I shake my head.
No.

Her chest collapses
back to normal,
her shoulders unhunch.
She is relieved.

I don't tell her that
I got a funny feeling

sometimes,
maybe the whole
last year.

A feeling like
something was
different
in how he looked
at me,
in the way
his touch
felt.

I don't tell her that
I kinda liked it.
That difference.
Like I was fun to be around.
Like I was growing up.

And now
that grown-up feeling
in my tummy
twists and turns

and wrings out
my insides.

And I feel like
a stupid kid.

Who should have known.

# THE PHONE CALL

I walk into the kitchen and
Mom's yelling and
pacing around.
*No, you can't talk to her!*
Mom screams into her phone.

*Who was THAT?* Tay asks when
Mom's done with the call,
still holding her phone,
staring at it like
she doesn't know what
to do with it.

*Grandma*, Mom says.

She finally sets the phone
down on the counter.

Tay and I look at each other.

Grandma?

# GRANDMA

Mom sits me down later
and explains
something that can't really
be explained.
How Grandma called to try and
talk us out of this "craziness,"
this idea that Uncle Andy
did something wrong,
that Mom's banished him,
that he can't ever
see me again.

Grandma doesn't believe
he did anything,
says he denied it
to the cops,
is mad they
even questioned him

after Mr. Jenkins told Mom
he was filing a report and
she agreed to be part of it.

*Of course he would deny it.*
Mom sighs, putting a hand
to her forehead
like she has a headache.

I don't remind Mom how
she thought that at first too:
her favorite, baby brother?
It had to be a mistake.

Mom says Grandma
thinks I'm too young
to understand,
that's why she thinks
I'm wrong and
he's right.

Mom says it calmly,
like they had discussed
it over tea.

But I remember her face
when she was screaming
into the phone.
Her face said what I feel now:

Grandma didn't choose us.

# LAILA

It *wasn't your fault*—
blah-blah-blah
—*wasn't your fault.*

It *wasn't your fault.*

That's about all
this lady can say,
this lady sitting
across from me:
a therapist
named Laila.
She looks about
the same age as
Tilda's older
sister who's a
teenager.

It wasn't your fault.

And this is what
she keeps saying
to me.
It wasn't my fault,
over and over.

And even though
she looks so young,
she says
It wasn't your fault
sitting up straight
as a tree trunk
across from me,
her eyes like a hawk's
holding mine,
their prey,
locked on hers.

It wasn't your fault.

And she means it.
It wasn't your fault.

Really means it.
It *wasn't your fault.*
She seems to know.
It *wasn't your fault.*
Like she's the Earth and
everything that goes on
is her domain.

Until...

Wait,
could Laila be
right?

# BUT THEN I REMEMBER ALL THE THINGS I DIDN'T TELL HER . . .

On the long car ride home,
the What-Ifs
start up again.

What if I'd paid attention
to the strange feeling in my gut,
to the weird look on his face?

What if I hadn't still been afraid
of being alone after school
and he hadn't been there at all?

What if I'd said,
That makes me uncomfortable, or
Stop it!
like you're supposed to . . .

and he had?

# RHEA AND MASON (AND ME)

Rhea and I are
at recess,
leaning up against
the brick wall.

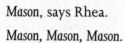

Mason, says Rhea.
Mason, Mason, Mason.

Mason is the boy she likes.

It must be cold out.
I can see my breath.

Mason, says Rhea.
Mason said he—

The door to the basement—
there it is
in my mind again.

*Mason*, says Rhea.

The stairs, the chipped paint on the walls going down.

*Don't you think that Mason . . . ?* says Rhea.
*Don't you think, Tori?*

Do I think? I think about the
battered, beat-up old couch,
the playing-around couch,
the stuffing coming out
that feels both rough and soft
when you poke at it
when you stare at it
when you want it to stop.
Cheap leather,
smooth on the edges but
cracking up
at the very center.

*Tori?* says Rhea.
She doesn't say
*Mason.*
*Tori?*

And suddenly I'm back,
brick wall at my back,
Rhea's face
inches away.

And her eyebrows are all
bunched up at me like
angry caterpillars.
*Tori! Why are you frowning like that?*
And her voice is all
porcupine-prickly and
mad at me.
*If you don't like him, then just say so!*
And she turns
away from me,
brown hair swishing,
and stomps off.

And I wonder how
we got into a fight
when I didn't
even hear
what she said.

# I FIGURE IT OUT

Taylor won't come down
to dinner tonight.
Mom tries a little
to coax her out of
her room, but then
lets Taylor be.

A few days ago
I overheard Mom
talking with Tay
about IT, asking
Tay if HE
ever touched her.
And He didn't so
I guess Mom's not
that worried
about Tay
being upset.

In my room later, though,
I'm staring at the wall,
trying as usual
not to think about It, when
something pokes at the edges
of my mind,
something shifts around stuck
in my chest,
like it's trying to roll a
a boulder.

Suddenly my big-sister antenna sense
kicks in
with a mind-picture of Tay in her room
alone
with this earthquake
that's jolting apart our family,
this bad thing that is
kind of
happening to her too.

And I know then
what I have to do.

# LET ME IN

Knock, knock.

My knuckles rap again, but there's
no Who's there? not
like when we used to tell jokes
till the milk went up our noses.
I stare at Taylor's closed door,
the KEEP OUT sign she
always has up,
even though she's never
meant it before.

Now it's different, and
I wonder how I'm going to
convince her to let me in.

It's me, I say to
the crack by the knob,

right up close
so she'll hear.

And I al-
most fall in-
to her room be-
cause the door op-
enssofast

# TAYLOR

Taylor's room is different
than I remember.
We haven't played much
the last couple years
(even before all this
happened).
The dolls and stuffed animals
that used to crowd her bed are
now just a few
favorites—
her tattered pink elephant,
her American Girl doll—
and there are some new
posters up—that singer
Mandy—hey, I like her too!

I must have seen this
all before, but now

it seems new,
like my little sister
standing there
looking at me
with serious eyes and
a pinched-up mouth.

She's not going to be the first
one to talk.

So here goes...

# SISTER SURPRISE

Somehow we end up
in sleeping bags
on the floor,
even though it's
only 7:30.

Somehow she ends up
understanding,
better than Mom,
even though she's
only eight.

# EMPTY

My dreams are haunted by
twitchy whiskers
a little pink nose
tiny furry feet.

I wake up one night in a cold sweat,
shovethatemptycage deep into my closet,
bury it under all my old soccer jerseys.

# SORRY

We're all late
for school
for work
Mom muttering
like she does
when she's stressed:
*the bank later—oh, an*
*accident—I'd better take*
*the back route—forgot*
*to tell Dan the report got*
*moved up—*

I toss my plate
into the sink,
half-eaten muffin
into the garbage
under the sink.

*Is that a leak?*
Mom screeches,
catching the cupboard
door before it closes.

Mom clasps her head
in dismay
at the water puddles
under the pipes—
*everything fall-*
*ing apart—I'll have to*
*ask Andy to—*

She stops midsentence
and looks at me,
horrified.
*What am I saying?*
she says, her tone chipper now,
almost jokey.
*We don't need any*
*Mr. Fix-Its. I can learn*
*to fix a leak. I'm going to*
*teach you girls—tonight!*

Tay groans.
I give a little nod,
duck my head,
and leave the room
so Mom can't see my face.

I catch a peek of
her sorry face
on my way out
and it makes me
feel even worse.

Mom doesn't have time
to fix the house.
She works
full-time,
overtime
since Dad left.
Now no more
Grandma to watch us,
no more help
with the house.

I feel bad
she has it so hard
because of what happened

because of me.

# SOCKS

I just can't find
them
my socks
I keep looking all
over
and it's
driving
me CRAZY
those socks
and I fling
everything
all over
my room
because I
can't
find them and
I haven't seen

Grandma
in over
a month
(*Grandma
promised He
won't be
there*, Mom said.
*She promised.*)
and it's
Thanksgiving
and we're
LATE
(COULD He
show up?
Will He
be there?)
Socks, must
focus on
my socks
Not in my
closet or
my drawers and
this is

going to
make us more
late late LATE
where are
those socks
where ARE
they?????

Then
all of a
sudden
Mom peeks
her head in the
door and
says, *What are you
doing, Tori?
We're la—*

And then she says,
*We won't go.*

Just like that.

And we don't.

And I don't
have to worry
about finding
my socks
anymore.

# NOT HERE

Tay's voice tugs at me
through my bedroom door,
an urgent whisper:
*Tori, Rhea's here,*
*she's right out front,*
*asking for you.*
But I'm under
covers again,
undercover
playing a girl
who isn't here.

*Tell her I'm not here.*

# GROWN-UPS ARE CRAZY

I hit a lamp off Laila's desk today
when she wouldn't leave IT alone
with the *And-how-do-you-feel-today?*
CRAP.

She clapped.

She said,
*Anger is good.*

This is news to me.

Tell that
to Ms. Radtke.

# MR. JENKINS'S LIE

Today we're having
a special presentation:
Beyond Stranger Danger.
My gut starts to squirm
as I realize what it's about.

*We don't only talk about*
*Stranger Danger anymore,*
say two ladies with
visitor name tags.
And it's like they read
my secret
from their clipboards:
*Kids are most likely*
*to be abused*
*by someone*
*they know well.*

A flush creeps up
my neck,
my face
starts to get hot.
Does anyone see me blushing?
And that awful thought makes it worse.
My cheeks burn,
stomach churns,
and my seat under me is a
gangplank
of doom.
I can barely keep
myself from squirming
all over.
But, please, don't let anyone see.

Then, suddenly,
as if the nightmare
in my mind has
slipped into the world:
my name
zings through the air.

But it's just Mr. Jenkins
saying,

Tori,
*I have a note here that you*
*are to go to the office.*
He slips it into my hand
and ushers me out the door.

I look at
the note that
sends me to the...

COUNSELOR'S office.

He wrote it himself.

So someone did notice.

Thank God for Mr. Jenkins.

# MEATLOAF CHAT

I pick up Mom's phone today, and
it's Grandma, and she sounds normal.

She talks to me about
meatloaf,
which is a typical
topic of conversation
for us.
How she wishes I
could taste the
one she's making,
it was Grandpa's
favorite, and
too bad Mom
has to be a
vegetarian
and never make it.

Then she says she
never sees me
anymore,
misses me,
wants to
see me.

Would like to
talk to me,
is sure she
could help
me to
under-
stand

what

hap—

I don't hear the
rest because I am

moving the phone
away from my ear.

And I feel kinda bad about it,
but I hang up on her.

# LOST

Nothing's really
fun anymore—
not like it used to be—
but I try
for Mom's sake
for Taylor's
to enjoy the Saturday
we drag out the boxes
and boxes
and boxes
of holiday decorations.
Everything's going
pretty well—tree up
and half done, all the old
favorites dangling:
the paper cutouts
that Mom loves,
mine the silver skate

Dad gave me,
Tay's kooky
scarfed squirrel.

And then my hand brushes
tissue paper and finds
a tiny stocking.
So cute and mini.
The one I always
insisted we put up
for Furball.
And my heart turns
into a lump in my chest,
in my throat.

I cover it back up
for someone else
to find
and tell Mom
I'm too tired
for any more fun today.

# GETTING BETTER

Mom checks on me later,
her cool hand touching
my forehead,
like when I'm sick
and she brings me Sprite
to settle my tummy,
or rubs Vicks on my chest
to help me breathe.

It'll *get better*, Mom says,
sitting there with me,
but her worried eyes
say something different
from her words.

Because how do you get better
when what happened
can't be fixed?

# A QUIET CHRISTMAS

Just the three of us.
Mom's not talking to Grandma again.
So I'll bet Uncle Andy's enjoying a nice
Christmas ham right now.

Just the three of us
in our house so quiet and steady
with mysterious clicks and tickings,
the rumbling of Tay's tummy
as we play endless Monopoly,
and the chanting prayer of Mom in the kitchen
swearing under her breath over the food.
Just the three of us,
making it
even though the food might be a disaster,
making it

without Grandma's ham.
Just the three of us.

And then Dad's
holiday call
erupts all over our
quiet Christmas.

# MAYBE I SHOULDN'T HAVE TOLD

*He was just so mad, Mom says.*
*Your dad isn't really going to*
*sue for custody.*
As if she doesn't look like she's
just been hit by a truck.
*He didn't really mean it.*
Like I won't notice how her voice
wobbles like Jell-O.

Mom says she should have told him
right away,
sooner;
she just kept putting it off.

I think maybe I shouldn't have told
him
her
anyone.

But I also think:
you can't protect someone from seven states away.
Dad must think he's some kind of superhero.
The kind where time and space don't matter.

Though maybe he's right.
He could've protected me,
come and checked things out—
EVER.
He could've gotten on a plane.

Or not gotten on one in the first place.

# PART THREE

# IS THAT ME?

I'm on my floor
looking,
looking at a girl
who's silly
(making bunny ears)
and goofy
(a half-cartwheel pose)
and good at choir
(fourth-grade regionals trophy).

Looking,
looking at a girl
with a best friend
(the heart charm Rhea gave me,
our county-fair pie win pic),
with an irritating sister
(more bunny ears),
and a look-alike mom.

I like that girl.

Did she leave forever?

I don't touch
the flipped-over
family reunion picture
on my bookshelf,
the one with cousins and great-aunts
and Him.

Because what if it answers:

Yes, she's gone.

# DAD'S REALLY HERE

A week later Dad picks me up
in a brand-new, bright red truck.
*How about that?*
he says way too merrily,
*It was the only rental they had left.*
*It's nice,* I say,
glancing over at Mom and Tay
as I step onto the sideboard.
Tay stares at the truck like she wants
to run her hands over it.
But I know she's just trying
not to look at Dad.
*Hey, Tay, you been a good girl?*
is all he's said to her.
His eyes seem to only
see me and avoid Mom's
hard-as-stone face,
which she always wears

just before exploding at Dad.
I climb in quick, swing my legs in.
*I'm bringing her back*, Dad tells Mom,
kinda snotty, through my open door.
*For now*, he adds, and I slam
the door shut fast before
more words start to fly.
*Let's go*, I say.
But I can't help
peeking back at Tay,
shoulders drooping,
flat hair falling in her face.
I know what she's thinking
because I would be thinking it too:
Dad didn't threaten not to bring HER back.

# THE STRANGER

*Remember how we always*
*played Bear Catcher?*
Dad says as he steers
through traffic.

I remember it.
Of course
I remember it.

> *Da-a-addy, I shriek, pretend-whiny,*
> *his nose nuzzling the top of my head,*
> *big, warm arms cuddling me close,*
> *eyes staring into mine,*
> *face delighted by me,*
> *by us.*

Now I stare at two long, hairy arms
I haven't touched in a year,

at a thin nose sniffing from the cold,
gaze sneaking from the windshield
to his charging phone,
the uneasy face of
a stranger to me.

And then I remember something,
remember that night years ago.
Of course.

*Remember that body-snatcher movie?*
I say because
it was real,
I just didn't
know it yet.

An alien really did take Dad over.

# BEV'S DINER

Sticky vinyl seats and
a junky old jukebox,
the yummiest
milkshakes in town.
And, right at the table,
a straw dispenser so
you can blow off wrappers,
as many as you want.

This is the place
of my memories,
the one we always
begged to go to,
Tay and me, though
she was just copying
me back then.
And it was the best

to go with just Daddy
on a special occasion.

Right now, at the booth
across from the prize machine,
that special-occasion feeling
bubbles up in me like it used to.

I blow a couple tops off straws.
I order a strawberry milkshake.
I stare out the window at a long-
forgotten paper blowing by...

*Do you want a quarter for a prize?*

...and I wonder how
I got here again,
this time with
the stranger
who doesn't know
how old almost-
eleven is.

# SHE'S OKAY

*Tell me what happened.*

I trace the wooden edge
of our booth, the barest sliver
separating us from the couple
eating right behind me who
I think I can hear
breathing—yikes—
that's how close they are.

*You can tell me, sweetheart.*

I need to tell him.
I need to be good
so he doesn't think
I'm having a problem.
I need to tell him
because maybe,

if I'm a good girl,
if he thinks, Hey,
*she's okay,*
*she's just fine,*
then he won't try
to take me away.

But I can't.

So instead
I order another
strawberry milkshake
even though I'm already
sick to my stomach
and ask Dad
about his new wife
Melanie
(like I care)
to distract him.

*Honey, tell me what happened*
*so I can understand, so I can*
*figure out what to do here.*

I *already told* Mom, I say.
And it's the wrong thing
to say because his eyes
retreat behind a cloud and
another thick block gets added
to the growing wall
between us.
All because I can't bring myself
to say It.

And yet he's here,
he IS.
Come to rescue me,
I guess.
It's hard to believe,
but he's really here.
So...


I get
a little bit
out
in a whisper:

what happened

in the basement

on the couch


My tiny words seem to smack Dad
in the face
and he finally stops asking.

# LUNCH MATH

Math's never been my favorite.
But what I really don't like is
lunch math.
Sometimes we still sit together,
Rhea and me. But even
addition's hard these days.

It would be easy if
the answer always
came out the same,
reliable,
like regular numbers,
instead of these always-
shifting
calculations of where to sit
and what to think about it.

Does 1 + 1 =
2 friends,
almost like before?
Before it became 2 =
1+1, together but apart,
for no good reason?

Or is it just endless
1+1 = 1+1
1 + 1 = 1 + 1
1 + 1 = 1 + 1
1      +      1 = 1      +      1
like each lonely one can't,
not ever again,
get together to make two?

# SCOOTING

I sit down next to Rhea today...
and she scoots
to make room.

      So I scoot.

But she scoots
again.
Scoot-

      scoot.

Scoot-

      scoot.

Scoot-

      scoo-

Sto-op! she says,
getting up and grabbing
the edges of her tray to move.

Oh.

*Wait!* I say, and
she looks so startled
to hear my voice that
she sits back down.

# BEST FRIEND BLOWUP

*Well?* says Rhea,
and I know enough not to
say, *Well, what?*
but I don't know
what TO say.

Rhea does.

YOU CAN'T JUST SIT THERE AND ACT LIKE
EVERYTHING'S NORMAL, TORI! YOU IGNORE ME,
AND THEN JUST EXPECT EVERYTHING TO BE THE
SAME? YOU TUNE OUT WHEN I'M TELLING YOU
STUFF—IMPORTANT STUFF! YOU PRETEND NOT TO
BE HOME WHEN I COME OVER—DON'T YOU DARE
DENY IT—I KNOW YOU WERE THERE! I MEAN,
WHAT AM I SUPPOSED TO THINK? DESTINY SAYS—

*Destiny?* I interrupt.

Your neighbor?
Because, of all the yucky things
Rhea's saying,
this name sticks like gum
on the shoe of my brain.
*The one who only talks*
*about nail polish?*

My eyes flick to Rhea's
rainbow sparkly nails that
I only just now notice.

*Yeah, well, at least she's*
*been there for me. SHE'S*
*not jealous of me liking Mason—*

                                        WHAT?!?

*—and SHE didn't leave me*
*stranded with no one*
*to trick-or-treat with*
*FOUR days before Halloween.*

                                        ??????????

You went trick-or-treating
with Destiny?
Something is not clicking

in my mind.
*Didn't she make fun of us*
*for that last year?*

Rhea sniffs and lifts her chin.
*She does happen to think*
*Halloween is more for*
*the early elementary crowd.*

Then—before I can stop myself—
*What, so*
*you just*
*painted your toenails*
*instead?*

That does it.

Rhea's up and out of there.

Based on the poisonous glare
she shoots me as she leaves,
I think I am lucky she takes
those rainbow nails with her.

# JEALOUS

California, I announce,
peeling off my special
faux-leather gloves,
flinging them carelessly
at the closet shelf,
*wouldn't require*
*so many clothes.*

Oh! says Mom.
*I forgot something!*
I pretend not to see
that she's crying as
she ducks back
into the kitchen
just as Tay comes out.

*Don't you see,* says Tay,
glaring at me as I take off my boots,

home from another diner date with Dad.
*Don't you see how*
*you're hurting Mom?*
*Acting like you'd be all excited to go*
*and live with Dad.*

A sting where my heart is, but
I don't want to feel it.
I liked Dad's stories
about California
and the beaches,
and even
a new baby brother,
which he makes sound
not-so-bad
even though
I should know better
from every single toddler
I've ever met.

I didn't even have to be
good this time.
I could just listen to him
and dream of

this problem-free
Fantasyland.
Besides, Disney's there,
I've never been, and
why should that baby
get to have all the fun?

*You're just jealous 'cause Dad's not trying to take you away!*

I clap my hands
over my mouth,
but it's too late.

Seems my voice has gone
lately from vanished
to wishing-it-would.

# A CLASSROOM LIST

One teacher:
straight-backed ruler of
expectations,
has-your-back defier of
expectations.

One old whiteboard:
past never fully erased,
haunting today's lessons with
marked-up ghost-streaks
from the day before
the day before
and the day before that.

One L-O-O-O-O-O-
O-O-O-O-ONG fluorescent light:
buzzing and flickering with
barely enough

energy to
make it
through the
day.

Twenty-eight kids:
looking out the window
looking at their hands
looking where they're supposed to . . .


. . . looking across the room at a friend
who used to be a friend
looking and wondering
looking and thinking
maybe it makes a little
bit of sense that
Rhea's mad.

# I TOLD HER!

I told Rhea
today at recess,
and it wasn't
weird!
Well, it was
weird.
But it wasn't
weird-weird.
I just took her
red-mittened hand
in my blue one
and pulled her over
to our place for
telling private stuff,
between the climbing wall
no one ever uses
(because of the spiders)

and the giant maple tree.
Rhea looked at me with her
eyebrows all the way up,
like what could I possibly
have to say to her now,
me looking around nervous
'cause the spot suddenly
didn't feel so hidden
with the big tree that bare.
But I took a breath and
did it anyway.

I didn't use the M-word
(which I hate;
it doesn't sound
like what It's
like, AT ALL).
I just said,
*I've been*
*acting weird,*
*huh?*
and she said,

Yeah, you have,
and I said, It's
because my uncle
did something
bad
to me.
And her eyes got
wi-i-i-de
and she got it,
she knew what I meant
right away.
I didn't even have
to say anything
else.

She grabbed my mittens
in her mittens
and gave them a squeeze.

And we just sat there for a while,
just comfortable together.

And THEN—

she started
talking about
Mason.

Well, I guess it IS
only a month
until Valentine's Day.

## AIR

Telling Rhea felt so good—
somehow so freeing—
like a boa constrictor
wrapped around my neck
finally letting go.

It feels so amazing now,
from telling her, that
something else buried deep
starts crawling its way up
to the surface of my mind,
where I kind of still don't want
to think about it.
But I also can't stand it
any longer:
those unexpected pangs to my heart
when that something rattles at me from

the glass container where I keep it
sealed up inside.

It's time to poke some holes in the jar
and give it some air.

# THE RAT

*What??!*
*I didn't know THAT!*
says Rhea,
when I mention
Furball's missing.
(I make it sound like
an accident.)


Rhea's been avoiding
the lunchroom kitchen
because of a little rat
she's seen scurrying by—

A rat that looks like . . .


Furball.

# GETTING HER BACK

Where could she be???!!!!!!!!
Which
crack
corner
crevice
holds Furball?


Does she know
I wish I could go
back in time,
change things,
not let her out?


Does she know
I didn't mean it,
that I love her,

even if HE
gave her to me?

These are the questions
on repeat,
the questions I ask
while we search,
Rhea and I—
together.

I also wonder about HER—
my best friend—who is suddenly
the sun shining on me.
And I didn't even realize
she'd been there all along,
right outside of
the cloud I was stuck in.

Can you be lonely

without knowing it?

Can you get someone back

when you didn't even know

she was lost?

# (NOT REALLY) FINE

On our fifth diner outing
Dad gets the call
I didn't know would come
until it did,
but then realized
I'd known the whole time
this would happen.

*Sorry, kiddo,*
his words too bright
in the dim light
of what he's saying.

A sick baby,
an emergency.
(A REAL emergency,
apparently.)
Melanie in hysterics,
calling him away.

He swings his phone around the joint
of his thumb and forefinger like
he does when he's nervous,
this stranger I know
so well and
not at all.

I'm only human,
the stranger says,
looking very sad.
I can't be in
two places
at once.

You're going NOW? Already?
Mom's sharp voice pierces through the phone
when he says we'll be back early,
on his way to the airport.
But I know this is good news
for her, his leaving,
his leaving me.

Never mind
the sinking feeling

in my tummy from him pulling
the plug on this diner daddy duo thing
that wasn't really real.

I need to remember
what's at stake.

Maybe if he forgets
about me again
I can stay home and
Mom will stop crying
when she thinks I can't see.

*Dad,* I say, neutral,
no hint of a whine,
no complaining,
*it's fine.*
My bright moment,
look at that good girl
so grown-up:
*I think you should go.*
*They need you there.*

# NOT UP TO ME

On the way back home
Detective Dad is back,
asks me to tell him if It
only happened That Once.
His voice is gentle,
it's the same question
Mom asked, but he
says I HAVE to tell him,
that he NEEDS to know.

And I—

                    *I don't want to live with you!!!!*

—LOSE it.

*Well, it's not up to you!*
Dad's face is red, but
his eyes look sorry.
He even follows

up with words:
*I shouldn't have*
*snapped at you.*

But he's right.
It never was
up to me:

Who lives where (across the entire country, that's
    where)
Who lives with him (his new family: Melanie and now
    that sick baby)
Who I live with (far away, not with him)
Who gets split up (Mom and Dad, me and Dad, Tay and
    Dad)

Being good is good for nothing:
it's never been up to me
and it never will be.
I may as well be a terror.
Being good doesn't help at all.

# THE GOOD GIRL

But when I see Mom's
pinched-up face waiting
for us in the driveway,
I try to get the good girl back—
FAST—
And I only slam the door shut
on his expensive rental truck
instead of kicking it.

# TAY AND ME

Later on, after
Dad's long gone,
I knock on Tay's door.

I stand there a minute,
trying to find the words
to apologize to
my baby sister
who stares at me
so serious like
she's aged twenty years
in a few weeks.

I'm *sorry*, I mumble,
but before I can say more,
about hogging Dad,
about stupidly having hope,
Tay stops me short.

I know, she says.

I get it.

But—I start up.

She cuts me off again.

You're not the one

who needs to say

Sorry.

# THE SEARCH

How could Furball
have gotten to
Treetop Elementary?!?

The backpack.
It's the only thing
we can think of,
Rhea and me.
Furball must have
somehow gotten into
my backpack.

We search and
we search and
we search but
no luck.

The kitchen,
the coatroom,
the rotten-mushroom-scented gym closet,
art.

Before school,
after school,
bathroom trips back inside at recess,
lunch.

Every
spare second
we have but
no luck.

My heart jumps
for a second when
something wriggles (!!)
on a card table jumbled
with toilet roll tunnels.

But this critter
belongs to a fourth-grade
science fair project:
someone else's pet.

# HOW OLD?

Maybe it's the cold, cold,
early March morning,
which makes the warm water running
down my back
        my arms
            my legs
feel so good,
like I'm going to melt
into a lounge chair
at the beach.

And somehow in my delicious state,
       for some unknowable reason in my vacationing
       mind,
old words from who knows back when—
Preschool?
Younger?
—start flowing out of my mouth.

*Grab your ducky,*
*start to hope.*
*Aren't you lucky?*
*You'll need your soap.*

Pouring out of me,
smooth and goofy.

I laugh and then start
the chorus:

*Bath-bath,*
*Bath, bathtime!*
*Bath-bath,*
*Bath, bathtime!*

The bathroom door opens
into a grinning Tay on my
towel-clad way out to my room.
She snorts at me.
*HOW old are you now?*

It's a dig I used to make at her,
when she'd throw a fit

at a restaurant or grocery store,
or anywhere else
that embarrassed me.
So I stick my tongue out at her,

which just makes her eyes twinkle
as she laughs at me some more.
*Seriously, Tay says,*
*What WAS that song?*

I pull the smaller towel off my hair
and whip it at her.
*Bathtime Bomp.*

# STILL WEIRD

I sassed Mom yesterday
about how fast
(okay, fine, how slow)
I cleared the table.

Her face got all
overripe tomato
like it does
when she's about
to explode.

And I felt a little jolt
of surprise 'cause
I haven't seen
that expression
in a while.
Guess this ghost girl's

been a model chore-do-er
what with my mind
distracted and my body
only half here.

But then instead of
flinging demands
and commands
and reprimands
(that was a challenge
spelling word last week),
Mom laughed
a short, barky laugh.
Her anger kind of
whooshed out
like when you let go
of the end of a balloon.

And then she laughed
some more.
And then I laughed too.
*She's back,* she said,
*my girl, I've missed her.*

And then I started crying
(tried to pretend I was
only laughing,
let my bangs fall over
my eyes)
because it all reminded me
how things are
Still
Weird.

# GUESS WHO?

When I get home from school today,
guess who's there in the living room?

Grandma's sitting on the sofa
facing the front door
when I come through it,
like she's been there all day,
waiting for me
to get home.

I am so
not in the mood
to talk about
meatloaf.

But she doesn't.
She just stretches both hands

out to me
and says,

I'm sorry.

# WHY GRANDMA'S HERE

It turns out
I wasn't the only one.
Another kid told on him.

It turns out
Uncle Andy got arrested.
He wants to get bailed out.

It turns out
that's why Grandma's here with me.
She came straight here instead.

# A START

It turns out
that "sorry" isn't the same
thing as back to normal.

When Grandma leaves,
I let her give me
a hug on her way
out the door past
Mom's tense face.
I can't melt into her hug—
not like before—though
it crushes my lungs
with her trying.
*I promise*
*to come back*
*again soon,*
she whispers

into my hair.

As Mom closes the door,
she looks at me with
a crooked almost-smile.
*Well, it's a start.*

# PART FOUR

# SPRINGTIME

When did the trees lose their leaves?

Now they have new buds. I see
how they look like thorns before
they unfurl as new leaves.

When did it get so cold?

Now it's warming up; I feel
my skin basking in the bright
sun toasting the cold air.

When did fall and winter come and go?

Now it is spring, and I hear
birds twittering like crazy,
eager to catch up, so much to do.

# WHAT THEN?

What if he goes to prison?

I shake my head clear, squint down at the work sheet in
front of me.

What if he doesn't?

Math's not really my thing, but I kind of like decimals.

What if I want him to?

They're so neat and tidy, their little dots telling you
everything you need to know.

What if I ~~never~~ see him again?

These
What-Ifs

will
make me
lose my mind,
lose my Self.
What if
I lose
the What-Ifs?

What then?

My pencil scratches, and I have
the answer.

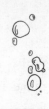

# THE OTHERS

How could I be glad?

That other kid,
who is she?
Or he?
Mom says now it's more,
more than one other kid
who's told.
Do they live near here,
maybe one street over,
on Magnolia Way?
Or far away from here,
maybe in Florida,
or New York City,
where He used to travel
for work sometimes?
Are they my age,

almost eleven,
just a couple short months
to make it official?

How could I be glad it
happened to them too?

I do feel bad for them,
I do. But...
But it means
I'm not crazy.
It means
I didn't lie.
It means
Grandma talked to me
about the ham she's
planning for Easter.
And Dad is finally
dropping his fight
for custody.
(Maybe he feels like
something got solved.
Probably he realized

he didn't really want
me to live with him and
his new family after all.)

But mainly it means
it wasn't just me.

How could that make me feel better?

I don't know.

But it does.

# NOT YET

Easter service today,
and there we were
at Grandma's church,
Mom guilted into going by
Grandma,
me and Tay dragged along by
Mom.

Just like I'd known it would be,
it was stare-at-a-fly-
for-excitement boring.

But then I was listening.
Looked away from that
fascinating fly,
looked up at Pastor Ríos

as he got going
about forgiveness.

But...I don't know.

He said all about
this Lamb
who does it all
for us.
We don't have to do
anything,
just let the Light shine
out from us.
The Lamb takes care
of the rest.
That's Forgiveness.

When he said that, I got a
yuck feeling like my
tummy would dribble right
down my legs and onto the
hard wooden pew.

I took a breath
(we were supposed
to be praying), and
I tried to let some Light in.
I peeked at
the stained-glass window
above Pastor Ríos.
And there was the Lamb.
A little baby Lamb.

But ... I don't know.

I didn't feel any sweet
Light there inside me.
Still just the sludgy yuck.

How can you forgive someone
you have been trying
not to think about
ever again?

I felt kind of bad about
feeling the yuck,
not the Light.

But then something in me said:

Not Yet.

And that felt
okay.

# A JOKE

Nate Young sits next to me now
that we've swapped desks for April.

He is the class clown.
I am a challenge.

Nate:
*How many tickles does it take*
*to make an octopus laugh?*

*Ten tickles. Get it? Ten-tacles?*

Very funny.

But it was. A little bit.

My cheeks hurt from smiling.

Guess I haven't used those muscles in a while.

# MAYBE

*It's so great to hear your voice!*
While I unlock my old purple bike from the rack,
Ms. Radkte walks over and smiles at me.
*Have you been singing again?*
I'm so startled by what she asks
that the noise coming from my throat stops.

Which is when I realize
I've been humming to myself
this whole time.

Um, I say.
I don't tell her about Bathtime Bomp.
Luckily she doesn't seem to need a real answer.
*Well, you're welcome to join in for*
*the spring concert if you want.*
Ms. Radkte sounds a little more

like her matter-of-fact teacher self now.
*We're doing two songs from last year.*

I manage a little nod. *Maybe.*

*I could even send a new song or two*
*home with you to practice.*

*Maybe.* I nod a little harder.

She gives me another non–Ms. Radkte smile,
then loses it fast as she catches sight
of some poor first grader running
wild rings around the HUG AND GO sign
and heads over to tell him off.

I turn back to my bike
and blow on its layer of dust.
When that doesn't work,
I swipe at it with my sweatshirt.

I hum all the way home.

# LOST AND FOUND

We are in the lunchroom kitchen,
sliding our trays onto a cart,
when I see something in the corner.
*What's that? What's that*
*brown spot over there?*

Oh, Tori, says Rhea.

# THE SPOT

Two steps,
four,
too many
more—
And there's the little brown
spot that isn't a spot
at all.

Rhea reaches out a hand—
Rhea who's so squeamish
she shrieks at worms on the
sidewalk after the rain—
Rhea touches Furball,
gently picks her up.

And I look—
I REALLY look—
at the tiny still body,

at the small helpless creature.
I look because I understand
that someone broke her, even though
she never did anything wrong.
I look because
I know I can't change
what's happened.
I look because
all I can do now
is caress her damp fur
with my tears.

# NO GOING BACK

I don't want another hamster,
I declare at dinner that night,
heading off Mom's likely
solution to my sad news.

What would I even name it?
Furball's the only good hamster
name, and it's already taken.
I know this isn't reasonable,
but I can't help it.
There can't be two Furballs.
There just can't.

Maybe we can get a dog,
I shouldn't promise, but . . .
Mom's voice is panicky and her eyes
dart around the room like she's trying
to figure out where she'd fit a dog in our

overstuffed kitchen with its in-the-way table
and counter crammed with cereal boxes.
*Yes-yes-yes-yes-yes*, Taylor chants.

No, I say, shaking my head. *It's okay, Mom.*
*It wouldn't be the same.*
*I don't want to replace her.*
Taylor glares at me like I've just given back
a trip to Disneyland, like why, why, WHY
would I EVER say that?

I shrug at her.
What CAN I say?
There's no going back.

# LAILA (FINALLY) CONVINCES ME TO TALK TO MOM

*Tori wants to share something*
*with you. Something that was*
*very hard for her when she*
*first told you about being*
*molested.*

Laila pauses and looks at me,
totally relaxed and patient,
like she could wait
in that moment
forever.

Mom coughs and looks at me,
her face all worried and tense,
like I'm about
to shoot her.

Okay, fine. I guess I'll put
her out of her misery.

I catch Laila's eye,
and she nods.
I take a deep breath,
and begin.

## BELIEVE ME, TAKE TWO

### (WITH A LITTLE HELP FROM LAILA)

She didn't—

You—you didn't—

*When I first*
*told you*
*about Uncle Andy,*

you didn't—
You said maybe I
Misunderstood—

Oh! But Tori, I—

You said he wouldn't—
*wouldn't ever*
*do that.*

(Tell her, not me.)

(Try to look at your mom.)

(It's okay, keep going.)

(Let her finish.)

Oh, Tori!

(Shh . . . hang on . . . you'll
get your chance.)

You didn't believe me,
not at first.

And then Mom's crying.

Oh, honey, and her tears
soak into my hair,
but I don't care.

I just didn't want it to
be true.

I didn't want it to
be true—
for you.

But I'm *so* glad you told me.

My baby . . .
And I let her hold me,
her baby.

# I'VE GOTTA ADMIT . . .

Laila's right sometimes.

# <u>LOTS</u> MORE MAYBES

Summer is all anyone
can talk about,
its sun shining on everyone
from

     5,

           4,

               3

                    weeks away,

dazzling them with dreams of
lazy mornings,
days stretched out so long,
late-night ice cream.


*Do you want to come*
*to Camp Aqua with me this year?*
Rhea asks.
*Maybe,* I say.
Camp is expensive.

*How about joining*
*Summer City Choir?*
Ms. Radkte proposes.
*Maybe, I say.*
*Probably yes.*

*I'd like you to consider*
*our summer mathletes program,*
Mr. Jenkins says.
*Um . . . okay, I say.*
Seriously?

But this summer bug hasn't
really infected me
until one day in May
Dad calls out of the blue
and says Tay and me
are invited to California for
the whole month of July.

*Wait. Can I talk to him?*
Mom snatches her phone back.
*This is the first I've heard.*
Mom turns red, then pale,

looks worried, then unhappy.
Tay and I shoot each other knowing glances
about how this is going to go.

But then—
The summer sun
shines its rays
all the way from July
across Mom's face
and she SMILES.
No, wait. Is she laughing?
Tay and I go googly-eyed.
*A break would be nice*, she says,
*thank Melanie for the idea*,
then hands the phone back to me.
Now our mouths drop open,
cartoon-style.

*So what do you think?*
Dad's voice is waiting on
my response,
My Choice.
*Maybe*, I say.
He still needs to

apologize to Tay—
and to me.
But the happiness
in my voice is clear.
*Good,* he replies.
*We'll keep talking*
*about it.*

The summer
waves hello
to me,
hopeful
that I'll join it
with all of its Maybes.

# WHY THAT OLD WIRE CAGE IS SITTING NEXT TO MY DESK AGAIN

It might seem weird,
digging it out of my closet now,
after it's too late.

I'm still sad when I look
at the empty cage, where sometimes
a shadow seems to move around,
nosing the purple food dish,
burrowing in a wood chip nest.
A dull ache in my chest throbs
along with this ghost-memory.

But I want to remember;
it doesn't haunt me.

It was trying to forget that did.

# MY UNCLE

My uncle,
I remember,
once picked me up.
I'd fallen down
roller-skating,
and he swooped in
and saved me
before I got
steamrolled
by all the other kids.
My uncle I remember.

My uncle,
I remember,
once picked me up.
I'd been alone
after school
and he drove up

and got me
because I got
forgotten
when my sister broke her arm.
My uncle I remember.

My uncle,
I remember,
spending time with him
was so easy.
I'd loved him all my life,
and then he did that
and changed things, and
made everything confusing.
Because I miss him on the days
when I remember my old uncle,
my uncle I can't forget.

# THE GIFT

A small, bright red present
from Rhea,
looking nervous,
as if she's going to vomit
like she used to back in preschool
when she got excited or
scared or mad or whatever.

We're gathered in the backyard,
my family and hers sitting
at the dingy old white plastic
picnic table.
(Rhea's wild-child brother,
Roan, is under the table,
animal-style.)

I peel off the paper,
pull off the lid.

Oh! Rhea,
she got me a...
But this hamster's
so different and
mousy looking,
its long snout sniffing.
It rocks back
on its hind legs
to stare at me.

Furball never did that.

# DIFFERENT

*But the only good name*
*for a hamster*
*is already gone....*
Taylor says in a hushed voice.
Then Roan pops out
from under the table,
for some reason only wearing
Superman underwear.
*That's a gwerbil!*
*I think he's right,* Mom says,
peering at the small gray
creature in my palm.
*Hamsters have shorter snouts.*
*And look at that tail!*

Oh, Rhea says, voice
trembly as the gerbil.
*I got it from a family.*

*I thought they knew.*
My fingers stroke the poor thing,
its heart beating life into my fingertips.
No, no, I say, trying to smile
at my sweet best friend.
*Gerbil can be her own hamster.*

*That's her name,* Tay screeches,
and she falls over in a giggling fit.
*Her name is Hamster!*

My lips curl in a smile.
And I feel ready,
ready to make new,
different memories
with Hamster the gerbil.

# A DAY LIKE TODAY

Do you think it's possible
to forget the most horrible,
terrible thing for hours at a time?


I laugh today, swinging up, up,
into the sky, Rhea in sync with me.


Do you think it's possible
to be happy in the middle of it all,
to feel your cheeks ache again with joy?


I run through the grass, which tickles
my feet and makes me laugh harder.


Do you think it's possible
to take a break from stale, recycled tears,
to gulp air fresher than a brand-new day?

I reach the front door, out of
breath,
from all that
running, from so much
laughing.

Do you think it's possible
to tie the dragging sadness to a tree
at the park, and leave it behind?

I shut the door behind me and there's the spot
on the carpet where he spilled coffee last summer.

And I remember, and
it comes back and
sinks its teeth into
my belly and won't let go.

But still.

A day like today . . .

It's possible.

I know that now.

# EPILOGUE

# THE LAST WORD

It's too late now
not to know
what I know.

And what I think—
what I know—
is that sometimes
you'll wish
you'd never heard
the words that,
put together,
make that horrible,
terrible poem
about what happened.

But you'll also know
that even though
the poem tells the truth,

it still didn't
have the last word.


You'll wake up one morning, and
you'll say YES to the day again.
And even if the sweetest
little rodent in the world
sometimes reminds you
of a darkness
you can't NOT see,
even then you will blink
your eyes clear.

You will wake and say
YES again—
if not that minute,
if not that day,
then the next—


And then
YOU
will have
The Last Word.

# AUTHOR'S NOTE

Five years ago, I was sitting out in the woods with a notebook when my main character Tori's voice came to tell me her story, starting with the poem "Believe Me." Since then, I have felt devoted to Tori's emerging voice and committed to shepherding this novel into the wider world.

Sexual abuse is—sadly, appallingly, unacceptably— a part of our world, and yet it can feel off-limits to speak about it. If you have been sexually abused and are unable to talk about it, then this silence about your own experience might cause you to feel ashamed or alone. Please know that you are not alone and that there are people who care about you and what happened to you. Following this author's note, there is a resources section with a list of organizations that can offer you help.

Even if you haven't been abused yourself, almost everyone (whether they are aware of it or not) knows someone who has experienced sexual abuse. Sometimes we assume, like Tori's friend Rhea in this novel, that someone's behavior has to do with a changing relationship, not realizing what they are going through. Even if we know what happened, it may be hard to understand what they are experiencing, and why they are reacting in certain ways. It can be difficult to imagine how much sexual abuse can affect many areas of a person's life. One of the best ways we can help someone is by listening to their story and believing them.

My hope for this book is that readers will be encouraged to tell their own truths, and—if someone doesn't believe them at first—to keep on telling until they get the help they need. Healing takes time. However, I personally know—along with countless other people around the world—that healing is not only possible, it IS where all of our stories are going.

# RESOURCES

For more information about sexual abuse, or to get help
for yourself or someone else, please contact:

StopItNow.org
1.888.PREVENT
(1.888.773.8368)

or
RAINN.org
1.800.656.HOPE
(1.800.656.4673)

For a state by state listing of other helpful organizations,
you can visit www.nsvrc.org.

# ACKNOWLEDGMENTS

My journey with this novel has been blessed with plentiful support along the way.

I want to start by thanking Phyllis Root and Gary Schmidt, who each provided invaluable encouragement and guidance in the earliest stages of the manuscript. Much gratitude goes out as well to the entire Hamline faculty and community for teaching me the skills essential to the writing life both on and off the page. Thank you to my class, the Max Fabs, for your friendship. It's a precious thing to connect deeply with others in as much joy and anguish over story as I am.

At Little, Brown Books for Young Readers, I'd like to thank the entire team, whose contributions have been essential to the final format of this book and to its introduction into the world: Michelle Campbell, Marisa Finkelstein, Bill Grace, Alexander Kelleher-Nagorski, Marcie Lawrence, Morgan Maple, Christie Michel, Emilie Polster, Victoria Stapleton, and Valerie Wong. To my editor,

Nikki Garcia: thank you for your spot-on literary prowess and for being such a wonderful champion of this book.

Thank you to my husband, Nick, and my children, Kai and Katja, for enabling me to persist, while staying grounded in life and relationship.

And, finally, though Tori's story is not my own journey, its heart and emotions wouldn't be possible without the work I've done processing my own trauma. I am grateful to the therapists, spiritual teachers, soul connections, friends, and family who have supported me along the way, as well as to those around the world who make it possible for—to paraphrase Leonard Cohen—the crack to let the light in.

ELC Photography

# SONJA K. SOLTER

graduated from Stanford University and earned an MFA in Writing for Children and Young Adults from Hamline University, with a critical thesis on writing trauma in middle-grade and young-adult realistic fiction. She is currently a creative writing mentor to youth with the Society of Young Inklings and enjoys writing poetry and prose for children of all ages. *When You Know What I Know* is her debut novel. Sonja lives with her husband and two children in Louisville, Colorado. She invites you to visit her at sonjaksolter.com.